"Exeter Waterfront" by Doris Rice

Exeter, New Hampshire...
where the river meets the tide

A Poetry Anthology

PublishingWorks • Exeter, NH • 2005

Copyright © 2005. Exeter Public Library. All rights reserved.

"Exeter Revisited" from *Collected Poems in English* by Joseph Brodsky. Copyright © 2000 by the Estate of Joseph Brodsky. Reprinted by permission of Farrar, Straus and Giroux, LLC.

A Sudden Gathering was originally published in a collection of poems entitled "A Bridge with a View" © 1997. Little Rabbit Press.

"Grapevine" © 1995 by the Christian Century Foundation. Reprinted by permission from the Christian Century, June 21-28, 1995.

"Tracks" - from *In the Orchard* (Tidal Press, 1986). First published in *Poetry*, September 1982. Note: The poem is based on a series of informal interviews with Exeter residents conducted during the summer of 1999.

 PublishingWorks • 4 Franklin Street • Exeter, NH 03833

ISBN: 1-933002-15-8

Book cover "String Bridge" by Helen Hazen

The majority of poems are arranged in alphabetical order by author. However, some are out of sequence to accommodate lengthy poems on facing pages and illustrations.

Printed in Canada

Contents
Authors

Abbott, Theresa
    Rose Spring, 13
Akins, Caroline Sutton
    Memorial Day in Exeter, 14
Albert, John-Michael
    King David of Exeter (fl. 1875-1885), 15
    Exeter, 16
Bell, Kaleigh
    Exeter's Night, 18
Boxold, R. D.
    Machine Dreams, 19
Brodsky, Joseph
    Exeter Revisited, 20
Buffington, Marion
    Tribute to an Unknown Exeter Woman, 21
Burlingham, Priscilla
    In Lieu of Fathers, 22
Carr, Mairead
    The Old Woman, 23
Chudleigh, Prudence
    Respect Starts with You, 24
Cooper, Ken
    RiverWoods' seasons, in haiku, 25
Daigle, Trina
    Down Near the Dock, 26
Darlington, Pam
    Summer Evening on the Squamscott, 27
Dewees, Anne
    Spring Prom, Exeter May 1947, 28
Dietz, Maggie
    North of Boston, 29
Ferguson, John
    Schooling, 30
Galle, Chuck
    A Day in Exeter, 32
Ganley, Lucretia Hess
    Major Blake's Hotel, 31

Gjettum, Pamela
    Ode to the Lamprey, 34
    Start at the Bandstand, 35
Goldberg, Midge
    The Bridge at Exeter, 36
Greene, Edith Leonard
    Team Play in Autumn, 37
Greer, Peter C.
    Aloofes, 38
Hackenson, Adele
    Memory Lane, 40
Hagen, Bill
    December Renaissance, 41
    The Tavern by the River's Edge, 42
Hennedy, Hugh
    Ferdinand and Miranda in Exeter, 43
    By the Squamscott in August, 44
Henson, Joan
    After Thanksgiving, on High Street, 46
    Used to be and Now, 47
Hill, Nancy Jean
    While Our Lungs are Collapsing, 48
Holder, Virginia
    Old Road, 50
Hubbe, Nancy
    Riverine Music, 52
Johnson, Gordon W.
    Snow in the Forecast, 54
Kellam, Dave
    Squamscott, 49
Leigh, Kate
    Wentworth Hall.....1957, 56
Mahoney, Sandra Tobin
    Front Street View, 57
Mann, Gary
    Gameday, 58
McCarthy, Jack
    Saltpetre and Robert Frost, 60

McGuinn, Rex
    On the Removal of the Diseased Elm from the Exeter Playing Fields, 59
    Shade on the Ice of the Exeter River, 62
McNeill, Barbara Tuxbury
    Water Street Bookstore, 63
Moore, Bob
    A Sudden Gathering, 64
Mousseau, Evan
    The dew and you, 66
Nelson, Karen
    Resting On the Academy Library Lawn, 67
Noonan, Karen
    Boards and Blades, 68
Nowak, Debra
    The Ioka Theatre, 70
    My Son Adam, 72
Parnell, Pat
    The Klan in Exeter, 71
    Cycling 101, 74
Pedrick, Jean
    Here, 75
Pelletier, Marsha
    the Legacy Behind the Man, 76
Pond, Gloria Dibble
    Exeter, 84
Pratt, Charles
    Grapevine, 77
    Tracks, 78
Reiter, Elizabeth
    Making Marks, 80
Rhodes, Ashley
    Raining, 79
Roberts, Ron
    River Tide, 82
Segal, Norma
    Boathouse, 86

Shepard, Harvey
    The Traces of History, 83
    Walking the Exeter Woods in Late Fall, 87

Smith, Charlene Mary-Cath
    Handkerchief Factory, 85
    on the Road from Manchester, 88

Supple, Colin
    Moe, 89

Tardiff, Olive
    Trolling for Ideas, 90

Tierney, Kelsey
    Daydreaming at the Beach, 91
    Layers of Magic, 92

Tirabassi, Maren C.
    At the Paloma Unit, 93

Weber, David
    Here and There: "Old Home Day,", 94

Whitney, Margaret Reed
    Market Day in Exeter, 95

Young, Donald R.
    The Most Mispronounced Word in Exeter, 96

Artists

Bouvron-Gromek, Annick
    " Autumn Colors", 84

Childs, Bill
    "String Bridge", 97

Clark, Kitty
    "Haunted Wood", 55

Cowan, Barbara
    "Along the Exeter River", 45

Hazen, Helen
    "String Bridge", Cover
    "Across the River", 86

Hubbe, Nancy
    "Riverine Music, Bird's Eye View", 53

McCarthy, Jane
    RiverWoods' seasons' Photograph, 25

Rice, Doris
    "Exeter Waterfront", Title page

Schweisberg, Sue
    "Waiting for the Alewives", 39

Veinot, Nick
    "603 Skate Club", 69

I have always considered poets to be so amazing; thier abiility to say so much in so few words is truly a gift.

Publishing an anthology of poems about our town of Exeter, New Hampshire enhanced by extraordinary illustrations seemed the best way for poets to share their gift.

Our poetry antholoogy is the outcome of a group effort, an anthology that would never have made it into print without everyone working together. I wish to thank the Exeter Public Library Board of Trustees for their continued support of the project. And I wish to thank all the library staff members for their help, direct and indirect.

I wish to thank the committee members: Annick Gromeck, Bob Moore, Deb Nowak, Harvey Shepard, Joan Henson, Pat Parnell, Sandra Mahoney, John Ferguson, and Pam Gjettum.

I also wish to thank the poets and illustrators for their original works of art.

Finally, I would like to give special acknowledgement to Denise DeLesDernier and Carol Guba for doing all of the really time consuming and sometimes daunting tasks needed to prepare the anthology for publication.

Hope F. Godino
Director, Exeter Public Library
2005

Exeter, New Hampshire...
*   where the river meets the tide*

A Poetry Anthology

Rose Spring
(Oak Street Extention, Exeter)
Theresa Abbott
Stratham, NH

I drive down the short, steep hill,
pull off to the right and take my place in line.
Two cars are ahead of me, windows open
this crisp September afternoon.
Sounds of a baseball game,
sportscaster's voice over organ music,
drift uphill.
A chipmunk on a nearby stone
chatters and scolds, complaining
of the intrusion.

A forty-something woman, bracelets jangling,
hands empty gallon jugs to a chubby boy
crouched at the spring's spout.
He fills and caps, fills and caps;
she reloads their car trunk.
My son's former high school shop teacher
leans against his car,
an empty cider jug dangling from each thumb.
We talk a while; he takes his turn and leaves.

I carry my crate of jugs to the spring
and repeat the ritual—
fill and cap, fill and cap.
A golden maple leaf, blown from
a nearby tree, spins in the catch basin.
Soon, the water splashing on the stone will freeze
and a thoughtful neighbor will remember
to bring a jug of sand.

We've turned our backs on Evian,
Poland Spring and Aquafina,
choosing Oak Street's cool clear flow—
liquid diamonds, tasting of sunlight, slightly salty.

As I cap the last jug, my hand
instinctively reaches to run off the tap.

Memorial Day in Exeter
Caroline Sutton Akins
Nashua, NH

Old men in uniforms parade in Exeter,
follow the flag that led them in war,
march with memories, keep step
with lingering shadows of silenced soldiers.

Politicians with banners, sidewalk faces,
children with bobbing balloons
blur as the soldiers focus on a crippled veteran
painfully standing, saluting his flag.

King David of Exeter (fl. 1875-1885)
John-Michael Albert
Dover, NH

Every village had its idiot. It wasn't pejorative, It was imperative. And bachelor uncles. Maiden aunts. Who else would teach the children their numbers or help with the haying? Or take a moment to watch the beavers in the river, or dole out advice to reckless squirrels in the street?

King David, in his coat-of-many-colors—he was homeless; his Bible was, by necessity, condensed – jingling down the street, deep in conversation with Himself. Smiling. Not particularly concerned with the way the mayor, or the preacher, or the sheriff think the world is supposed to be.

But King David was necessary. How else were the children to know that they should revel in difference, that they had options beyond the *dicta* of their parents?

Exeter

John-Michael Albert
Dover, NH

Twenty-minutes' tunneling through trees
on the train from Dover to Exeter;
New Hampshire woods in August:
thick with silver fog and green shade.

The regular metallic click, the low rumble
of touristy conversation: English painted
in a thick, East European palate.
The woods open onto dark ponds:
duckweed and ninuphars;
and then the flat expanse of the Squamscott,
a brackish estuary, a tidal marriage
of the Gulf of Maine and the Exeter River
strafed by squadrons of tiny terns.

To a walker, these streets have no names,
Only character: the service stations
   (still offering service)
the flower shop, the bakery, the gangly
yellow compound on the hill, the music store,
three book stores
   (two new and one antique)
the pregnant Italian restaurant, bulging green
into the library road, and always, the Dam View Café
for Irish Benedict, coffee, home fries,
and tree swallows
   (outside the window)
scribbling mutable messages on the mirrored
surface of the static waters above the dam.

        Exeter,
   I first knew you at thirteen,
    as an Ohio farm boy,
finding myself in Leper Lepelier's
     Separate Peace.
     You taught me
   the mollifying grace
of Beauty acting on Horror.
Later, my University, Sewanee,

perched on the Cumberland Plateau
in Tennessee,
taught me that places like you
really *do* exist.

And four years ago,
when I moved to New Hampshire,
Antoinetta told me over Chinese,
"Knowles's diving tree is real.
It still stretches out over the Exeter River."
Exeter, it was as if an angel chose
a fast-food moment, to whisper in my ear,
like and annunciation,
that Eden is still here, as is The Tree.

I get here when the train gets here;
I leave when it leaves. I recommend it.

You surrendered your tall, straight pines
for masts and rolling fields,
for hay and sheep.
You milled Southern cotton into sheets
and Northern wool into blue uniforms.
You nurtured the bairns of the rich
and sent them out to dream
of a fabled city by the sea.

From the benches by the buoyed boats,
I study your stretch of grim red mills
(now chi-chi apartments)
crowding the Squamscott bank for blocks,
anonymous yuppie windows
open to the conversant chits and chirrs
of red-winged blackbirds nesting,
unseen,
among the chest-high sedges
and the dark green reeds.

Exeter's Night
Kaleigh Bell
Holland Landing, Ontario

Wildly, the playful moon towers above me, the ground.
Troubled and gloomy, I shut down.
All is quiet.
I hear the giggles of the playful stars in the mellow sky.
The muted colors of the sky leave a peaceful pallet.
Exeter's Night.

Machine Dreams
09/30/99
R.D. Boxold
Plaistow, NH

The time has come,
to close the door,
To turn the lock,
for forever more.
At the place you spent,
so many days,
And turn your mind,
to different ways.

Trace back now
over time,
To a different economic
clime,
When a man could build
with blood and sweat,
And give his time
without regret.
To have what's yours,
until it's end,
No merger or buy-out,
fate to rend.

To lock the door
and walk away,
Alone to face a
brand new day.
To end the thing that
you had wrought,
And pass on alone,
From your loyal court.

In tribute to the now deceased resident of Exeter, Robert Barney. Mr. Barney was the former owner of the Hampton Machine Company which closed its doors for good on 09/30/99.

Exeter Revisited
Joseph Brodsky

Playing chess on the oil tablecloth at Sparky's
Café, with half & half for whites,
against your specter at noon, two flights
down from that mattress, and seven years later. Scarcely
a gambit, by any standard. The fan's dust-plagued
shamrock still hums in your window—seven
years later and pints of semen
Under the bridge—apparently not unplugged.
What does it take to pledge allegiance
to another biography, ocean, creed?
The expiration date on the Indian Deed?
A pair of turtledoves, two young pigeons?
The Atlantic, whose long-brewed invasion looks,
on the beaches of Salisbury, self-defeating?
Or the town hall cupola, still breast-feeding
its pale, cloud-swaddled Lux?

Joseph Brodsky (1940-1996) was born in Leningrad and came to the United States in 1972, an involuntary exile from the Soviet Union. He taught at many colleges, including Columbia, the University of Michigan, and Mount Holyoke. He received the Nobel Prize in Literature in 1987 and was Poet Laureate of the United States in 1991 and 1992. When Brodsky wrote *Exeter Revisited*, Sparky's Café was located at the corner of Water Street and String Bridge (where Sal & Anthony's restaurant is presently located).

Tribute to an Unknown Exeter Woman
Circa 1938
Marion Buffington
Raymond, NH

Just now, like a candle floating on a rippled pond,
    lighting up the night,
your image slipped into memory, more real than the
    sole, brief time I saw you:
there, on Water Street near String Bridge,
    while I waited for Grandmother.

You were walking quietly along, enfolded to the ankles
    in a dark coat, the color of unmined gold,
your form slowed and slanted to the town's steep hill,
    a column braced against the coming climb.
You seemed greedless for the world's thousand things
    that vanish to the touch.

For an instant you paused, and I from my child-face
    looked up to you, grey as time,
and beheld the hurt in your flint-fired eyes,
    a mirror of mine:
Suddenly you smiled, kindness falling soft as feathers
    from your face to mine.

In Lieu Of Fathers
Priscilla Burlingham
Moultonborough, NH

Our heroes were horses with names like
Man Of War and War Admiral
We memorized with fervor every
part of their anatomy and
searched each horse we saw for
"The Look Of Eagles"

Lineage was in the front of
our eight year old minds
along with gait and confirmation
and the primal wish to ride
bare-back through the ghostly veils
of loving and looking for our fathers

There was a war somewhere
it took fathers away but not
the horses
we pinned our father's names
next to champions sired by Man Of War
we read horse books right in the stalls
the letters from overseas stopped
and slowly, slowly the barn became
the foster home

And fathers who didn't write
were just a name…mine returned
a stranger who didn't like horses
and he didn't look free
at least not the way a horse looks
when running a full field at liberty

Secretly disappointed, I took my
father's name down
and told him by explanation
that he didn't have "The Look Of Eagles"
he didn't know what I meant
and I don't remember feeling revenge
it simply seemed the right thing to do

The Old Woman
Mairead Carr
Exeter Student

One day in July cool and warm,
I climbed up an old woman bent with age.
The wind blew through her old ragged hair,
But still I climbed on her gnarled arms that reached out to the sky.

When I reached her hunched shoulders,
I paused and asked this ancient figure,
"Old woman, how long have you stood here and watched the sun rise and set?"
"How long have you enlightened us with your wisdom and hidden beauty?"

I sat in silence waiting for answer,
The only sound was the wind blowing against us.
Ages passed and flowers bloomed, but still I had no answer.
Then autumn came and pieces of the old woman's hair began to fall.

By winter the old woman was bare
Snow began to fall and bend her arms down toward earth.
The icy frost chilled me so that I had to leave to return in spring.
That winter seemed to last only to keep me away longer.

Finally, spring arrived knocking at my door,
And I ran with wings towards the old woman that had stood alone.
Where I thought to see the old woman standing in serenity, I spied only a stump.
And carved in that stump were the words, "Not Long Enough."

Respect Starts with You
Prudence Chudleigh
Exeter, NH

Listen, grizzled gray, sebum-flaked tom cat,

That was a son and granddaughter

You nearly smashed flat backing out

With your not-so-new dirty Cadillac.

When you buddy yaowl

At the local Legion bar

About young squirts today

Showing no respect for old soldiers,

Remember, you grunts

Failed to honor the Town's W.W. II cannon

With names of servicemen and women,

Up-rooted from old County/Town Hall then

Misplaced, abandoned, lost, almost forgotten.

You want respect? Show us.

You want manners? Teach us.

RiverWoods' seasons, in haiku

Ken Cooper
Exeter, NH

Snow is Winter's gift.
Three inches is most welcome,
Three feet is much less.

In heavy Spring rains
Earthworms try to cross the road.
They seldom make it.

Summer is quite hot
And not much fun except for
Air conditioning.

Fall in New England
With its beautiful colors
We wait for all year.

Photograph by Jane McCarty

Down Near the Dock
Trina Daigle
Newmarket, NH

This sun-locked, long wood dock, dotted with gull disorder, peck and rot,
floats not far from the falls, where fresh water turns,
then churns to salt brine flow and dark. Nearby, tied with line,
the megaphone motor boats sulk to the side and wait for coach and crew.
The wide blue is September, water and air.

Down below sifts black silt through eels' slipknots
where currents turn them around straight into a heron's gullet.
This is where high tides mark granite block wall, the chain link fence,
small shrubs with a wash of pressed leaves, socks and grass.
This is where those who come to pass the hour, who wish to walk,
roll their wheels, or take great strides upon the heels
of illegal dog and laughing runaway child.

This is the place where those who come to look within,
latch arms upon a whim and watch the wake rowers make mile after unseen mile.
Shoreline lovers lean into each other as first team comes up to dock.
Scuff and weight, drip and print make wood what it is upon the water.
They come again with sculls and oars to stretch farther than before.
Again they come to bend at waist and knee, pull through turn and weed,
to row the pace, and glide the scull away from edge to sea, from sea to edge.
They come to wet their feet, set the beat, feel the heart heat, breath of another.

This is the place where river's bend and tow give warmth to chilled air
the charms to row through witch's hair that curls as she combs and rises.
Last chance to feel their bodies charge, their wake as one. The halls are warmer.
A season's race is over where below the beam the sculls suspend
within the hush of light, the ramps are pulled, the dock erased,
the blackened current lulled to sleep
and fishermen wait for ice.

Summer Evening on the Squamscott
Pam Darlington
Hampton Falls, NH

I leave the town landing, tired and discouraged.
After my workday, I need to be out
On the river alone; no one around me.
Town noises vanish as I paddle along.

Alone in my kayak; tide pulls me ahead.
It's dinnertime; no one else is about.
Water dark blue, rippling behind me;
Ahead of me, sparkling from shore to shore.

I feel less frantic; my head starts to clear.
Paddle strokes slow; my eyes can now focus.
Relaxing, finally seeing the river and shoreline.
I find my own rhythm, churning ahead.

I see dark shore grasses, twisting and green,
Eelgrass, brown, floating with the current,
Insects and birds, searching the near shoreline,
Eddies of water, in constant motion

My kayak moves slowly, the sun sinks down low;
Colors changing now, are muted and dull.
Turning around, I head back towards the landing.
I have to pull harder; tide is against me.

Turn the last bend in the river by Swasey,
The windows are lighted; streetlights are on.
Headlights twinkle as darkness descends and
Away from the water, shadows abound.

I push towards the landing; my mind is now clear.
Ready to go back to my life and my work.
My boat slows quickly; no forward motion.
I hear…silence, see…darkness. Time to go home.

Spring Poem, Exeter, May 1947

Anne Dewees
Portsmouth, NH

In Thompson Gym,
the swimming pool became the Mississippi,
a giant backdrop depicted a plantation,
a riverside wharf, a side wheeler.

So long ago,
but she could still remember
the evening, Peter,
a satin petalled gardenia.

They jitterbugged to IN THE MOOD,
danced the foxtrot under watchful eyes.
But with the first notes of MOONLIGHT SERENADE,
his white gloved palm pressed her close.
Cheek to cheek, they swayed,
essence of gardenia, starched shirt,
mingled with arousal.

At intermission, they flowed out
into leafy shadow, the edge of darkness,
trembling with joy and terror,
from the night, the touch,
the moonlight serenade.

North of Boston

Maggie Dietz
Exeter, NH

Hoarfrost coats and cuffs
the playing fields, a heyday
of glistening. So there's hope
in my throat as I walk across them
to the woods with my chest
flung open, spilling its coins.
The light so bright I can hear it,
a silver tone like a penny whistle.

It's fall, so I'm craving pine cones.
Hundreds of maples the color
of bulldozers!

     But something strange
is going on: the trees are tired
of meaning, sick of providing
mystery, parallels, consolation.
"Leave us alone" they seem to cry,
with barely energy for a pun.

The muscular river crawls on
its belly in a maple coat of mail.
Muddy and unreflective, it smells
as if it too could use some privacy.

The sumac reddens like a face,
holding out its velvet pods
almost desperately. The Queen
Anne's Lace clicks in the wind.

A deaf-mute milkweed,
foaming at the mouth.

Back at the field, I look
for what I didn't mean
to drop. The grass is green.

     Okay, Day,
my host, I want to get out
of your house. Come on, Night,
with your twinkly stars and big
dumb moon. Tell me don't
show me, and wipe that grin
off your face.

Schooling

John Ferguson
Portsmouth, NH

I took my class on a field trip
To Swasey Parkway
I lowered them carefully
Into the Squamscott

For a moment
They were a school
Alphabetically arranged
Anticipating

Then eddies and currents
Dispersed them
Some fought upstream
Others went with the flow

I took my shoes off
Settled on the bank
With a book of poems
For the afternoon

The train raced behind me
The sun moved in the sky
I read some verse
And waited for my fries

I waited patiently
The moon replaced the sun
I found my shoes and sweater
And walked back to the school

I guess that's what we do
Year after year
We send them off
Into a fluid world

I guess that's what I want
That none return
That they find their own world
Wherever they swim

Major Blake's Hotel

Lucretia Hess Ganley
Exeter, NH

Three on an elevator, nose to nose,
Backs to boxes, toes to toes

Half a ton the maximum weight
We and cartons make the freight.

Slowly upward comes our floor,
Heavy boxes out the door.

Tug and lug them up the stair
Want and need, a powerful pair.

Drag the pieces through the door
Lay them out upon the floor.

Parts A & B, slide into C,
Bolt and lock nut fit hole D.

Assemble a desk, then a chair,
Furnish a room out of thin air.

A sweet retreat, a private place
To meet with clients face to face.

A place to heal and counsel all
Fourth floor corner, end of hall.

A Day in Exeter
Chuck Galle
Greenland, NH

What I wonder is: Were there some people
among the founders of this little town
who left the county seat of Devonshire?
Or was there some other reason for them
to relocate that name from there to here?
Two cities on two rivers, that's a good
connection also; a bit of jolly
empire for a Lincoln-bred Puritan,
one might think. At any rate when Wheelwright
down in Wollaston stood firmly for his
view of God and Man, and defended Anne
Hutchison (and wed her sister right there
before God and everybody), those God-
loving Christians drove him from the Bay state.
The Squamscott River confluence from fresh
water seemed the place to practice freely.

Sixteen thirty-eight. Among the first four
townships in the colony New Hampshire.
Water power flowed in great abundance;
grains, wood flax seed, wool for fulling, all were
grist for the mills which fell upon the falls
enriching commerce in this hard new world.
So stately was its posture, so rugged
its constitution, so conventional
its seat of governance the capital
was centered here. For fourteen years. And then,
and then, they gave some other towns the chance.

A grove of Elms and Ash Bow South toward
the Forest of Maple, Chestnut and Pine;
a Bittersweet but Pleasant view of Green
Park land where Robins and Whippoorwills fly
finding occasional Linden, Alder
and Cherry. Once saw Mills Fronted on the
Water, the Main source of business in town.
And that Gilman lad was certainly a
treasure. I poke around in a silly
old room with uneven walls and rolling

floors. Around the corner I hear gallant
jazz ghosts wail and trickle, bob and quaver.
Timeless town, a year's worth of days years old,
nestled and sculpted into the river
winding to the old Great Bay, sparkling fresh
spilling into brackish, the city once
a port is now portal to history.

We search the town and find some adventures;
a basket seine-caster catching alewives,
a pumpkin-cannon maker speaks to our
willing ears and tells us about whales
and of upstream spawners needing man-made
steps – elevators to bypass blockades
against their progenic destination.
Further down the now-named Squamscott River
we snatch the double falls framed in the arch
within our intrepid long-eyed camera.
We also catch a handmade lunch at The
Tavern At The Rivers Edge – to take out.
With wholesome sandwiches and iced tea, we
lunch looking at the old wood motor launch.
(Didn't they use to have them at the Weirs?)
A cormorant, tucked back and skimming low,
soars along without fluttering a wing
and joins his fellow dancers on a rock.
Later, we walk the Exeter River,
a huge cannon points but does not aim
at children swimming on the other side,
large yellow flowers nod on the surface.
And then the day is done and out beyond
Old Dame Justice, raised atop the town hall
standing proudly in its light, the glaring
sun rides off slowly into all the West.

Ode to the Lamprey

Pamela Gjettum
Exeter, NH

The Lamprey is a river
The lamprey is an eel.
The eels are all a-quiver,
The eelers full of zeal.

People used to eat them
They thought them quite a treat;
They'd boil them up or fry them
As something good to eat.

When I first came to Exeter
The eels began to die.
Their bodies slimed the water;
It made you want to cry.

Dead eels are not a pretty sight;
They're fat and tubular
And when they're dying all at once
They blanket the river.

King Henry died from eating eels
A dish that's fit for kings;
I thought I'd die from smelling them,
The nasty stinking things.

Start at the Bandstand
Pamela Gjettum
Exeter, NH

How do I get there? *Start at the Bandstand.*
Everything in Exeter starts at the bandstand,
Parades start there. The road race and the bike race,
They start there.

The town offices are there. The old town hall,
With its white columns (they were once a kind of mauve)
And tall lady Justice (once some kids climbed up
And gave her a red flannel skirt) that's there at the bandstand.

They still have band concerts there in the summer,
Broadway tunes wavering against the traffic
While peoples sit in their cars and honk to applaud.
Civic groups hold sales there. Kiwanis roasts
Hot dogs there twice a year while Rotary
Sells apples and apple pies.

There's an inn there, called The Inn at the Bandstand,
With a friendly guard dog who sleeps on the sidewalk.
People feed him bits of doughnut
As they step over him, coming out of the coffee shop.

You can park at the bandstand, with cars
Lined up in the middle of the street,
From there it's an easy walk to anywhere
In town: the library, the IOKA theater,
Water Street Books.

A lot of stores have closed. There used
To be a Woolworths, where you could get
Anything. There was Poggio's market
With fresh fruit and vegetables and groceries inside.
There was Kennedy's for milk and meat and butter.
You could get clothes, and shoes and office
Supplies. Now you get lawyers and gifts.

At Christmas the bandstand is a halo of lights
Sparking in the snow. Santa Claus starts at the bandstand.

Start at the bandstand. You will start at the bandstand, in Exeter.
You just don't get as far as you used to.

The Bridge at Exeter
Midge Goldberg
Derry, NH

At MIT, they used an Oliver Smoot,
A freshman there, and stretched him end to end
To see how many Smoots make up one bridge.
At Exeter there was a boy, Tom Paks,
Who being short and drunk, thought he should be
The ruler measuring the bridge in town.
He lay down on the concrete wall one night
But could not find a measuring tape to use.
He did not understand that Tom would be
The unit, all contained within himself,
By which to measure footsteps passing by.
The equation's inverse that he had to solve
To start to span beyond the measured feet:
How many bridges make a Paks complete?

Team Play in Autumn

Edith Leonard Greene
Center Harbor, NH

Wind shakes leaves loose to encounter the air,
Over the soccer field, flung with a flare;
Eleven in scarlet, eleven in gold,
Bare arms and legs making nothing of cold.

Tossed with the wind, or the turn of the ball,
Leaping to check it and counter its fall,
With a twist of the body, a thrust of the head,
Till the soccer ball soars where the green has all fled.

Now over the gold of the day comes the dimming
Sad grey of November: October's sun swimming
Downward to this. The last goal is won
And colored scraps scatter when soccer is done.

Next fall on the playing field, sun will slant through,
Angled like this, for the deep gold and true
That tells of another year turning toward cold
And the game never ended, although players grow old.

Aloofes

Peter C. Greer
Exeter, NH

Before the Squamscott was the Squamscott,
before Spring was Spring or May May,
before even the Earth was the Earth,
when the sun's light reached the right angle,
they swam out of the wide brine of the sea
into a funnel of streaming and freshening water
in search of an eddy sweet and still enough
to harbor eggs. And one day, they were alewives.

Daily now, I walk a bank of the Squamscott,
then cross a bridge that was not there before,
to watch the water from a river of a different
name slip over dams that were not there before,
and listen as it roars over rocks that beat
to a froth the fresh blending with the salt.
Anadromous I've learned those alewives are,
and in our May they run upstream to spawn.

Before they were alewives, they were, some say,
aloofes, named so by people ruddier than I,
and more savvy in the ways of water and fish.
Long before my ancestors farmed the land
drained by this river, those people cast their nets
to catch *aloofes* for uses best known to them.
Now, on my walks, I witness folks like me
netting alewives to use as bait for bass.

Why, I wonder, do I prefer *aloofes* to alewives?
Am I drawn to the darker skin and prime ways
of those whose lips first formed the word?
Am I called by the time when the native river
flowed unbroken from a sweet source
into an endless ocean? Or do I simply love
the lesson, through a name strange to my ears,
that life runs before the names that we must give it?

"Waiting for the Alewives" by Sue Schweisberg

Memory Lane
Adele Hackenson
Framingham, MA

Quaint little Exeter, my mother's hometown

She spoke of it often as a place of renown.

As the years went along I was privileged to share

Many summers in Exeter with relatives there.

The IOKA theater provided Saturday's fun

And the two nearby beaches gave us fun in the sun.

"COZY CORNER", the place where good friends went to meet

And exchange local gossip and then have a treat.

The rambling old shoe shop kept many alive

In a time of depression when it was hard to survive.

The streets, Myrtle and Sanborn, a small ethnic village

Doors always open…there was no fear of pillage.

As I visit there now, lingering memories I treasure

Of my days spent in Exeter that gave me so much pleasure.

December Renaissance
Bill Hagen
Exeter, NH

Twelve below: sea smoke
Billows on the coastline.
My beard a thatch of frozen breath;
The squeak of air cured snow
Accents the void of tree and field.
I have soaked up the cold all day.
Your west coast calls,
Your voice singing the wire,
Ringing oceans away
Sharp as the February sun
Ignites a memory:
The shadow of your form.
You move in my space:
Over Loaf and Ladle coffee,
Those Botticelli eyes,
Half-lidded, North Sea blue-
This is the face I will Love…

The Tavern by the River's Edge
Bill Hagen
Exeter, NH

Huddled and walking fast
Along the ice filled street
Then down a narrow flight
Into a cloistered bar
Humming with laughter
And the late news.

Cradled in my high back stool
Chris, Tom and Jenn
Cash up the day:
The last hour, the last call:
Jenn laughing reaches
To squeeze my hand.

I butt my smoke
Slide into my coat
Tomorrow's rituals drumming
Faintly in my head.
Then back through the darkness to another day.

Wet snow tonight
Freezing rain at dawn;
The heavy sky
Motionless, poised, waiting.

Ferdinand and Miranda in Exeter
for John and Joan Henson

Hugh Hennedy
Portsmouth, NH

Retired to their den
They play chess
She learning
He letting
His body heal
She happy
To learn and lose
Not having lost him

Mastery
Of self and other
No longer a problem
O brave new world
That has such tested
Soulship in it

By the Squamscott in August
Hugh Hennedy
Portsmouth, NH

Peeps drilling on the flats
and the blue bands
edged with white
of the small brown ducks
taken at first as female mallards

Flying across and hovering over
the river a kingfisher
a few gulls
lots of sparrows filling the voids
of the wire fence and near bushes

Starlings on the grass
from which a mockingbird flies
to a tree not
dedicated to the dead
a lone robin

On the walk with me
whitehaired women walking their glasses
and three children on bikes
followed at some distance
by a mother on foot

"Along the Exeter River" by Barbara Cowan

After Thanksgiving, on High Street

Joan Henson
Exeter, NH

In town, at the window—
leavings of family still
blessing our kitchen

As crumbs on the table
and pans and platters
piled shining

On counters and stove—
happy to sip my coffee
watching the cold outside

Testing for ways to get in
icicles clinging
like teeth to the eaves

House and me
both lazy this morning
dressed in an early sky

The clouds not clouds
but one long breath
on a shortening day

Tipping my cup
to these last hours
of November

    Yesterday gone
    today already
    a ghost of tomorrow

    Remember remember
    all of this all of this

    Hold

Used to be and Now

Joan Henson
Exeter, NH

Once you could take the trolley from my corner
to Portsmouth or even better to Hampton Beach—
trolleys clanging to neighborhoods older than ours, relatives,
weddings and funerals or much better! bringing home
bonneted mothers with empty food baskets
balancing children whiny with red faces
and sand in their toes.

Families, sons, daughters, grandchildren come by
here to tell us how it was in their time or what they
remember of here and then. Each time, we learn more.
Of course the house holds it all. Down in the cellar
someone wrote on a chalkboard the owner, C.J.
Watson, and date, 1888—perhaps the builder. We
know there was once a wraparound porch from the
front of the house to the shed.
And the house next door had no out-of-scale dormers;
instead, it looked much like ours—they were two sisters
in tune with each other, kinship between them proper to street
and the people who strolled or lived on it.

Used to be one other wall in our library room, a sofa and
rocking chair, warm from the stove, in our kitchen.
Used to be flowers and vegetable gardens filling the side yard!
With fruit trees, pear and plum; and those strangely set flagstones
half-buried in grass, that walk from the driveway down to that yard,
stopping smack in the middle, with no seeming purpose, once led
to a large fountain. Grandchildren long before ours remember
Its grandeur and spray. Those really are grape vines crawling
from under the deck we put up—what remains of an arbor
and Concords, just as my grandfather had in Portsmouth.

Three sets of strangers from Rye, Connecticut, Oregon, slowing
and finally, timidly, stopping by. Knocking.
Since we all have our own lost houses, we let them in.
Let them climb the back stairs, go through to the rear of the house
beyond the main bathroom, through the ghost of a fifth room we
never knew was there and open the door to the loft and sniff—
and tell us it still smells like home.

While Our Lungs are Collapsing
Nancy Jean Hill
Plymouth, NH

I remember your eyes, full
of fury. You'd been ranting
about Dad. Suddenly, you couldn't
breathe. I carried you, light and limp,
still ranting, down three flights,
placed you in my Subaru and drove
along 101 C, cursing at drivers
obeying the speed limit while you
grabbed air with one lung
and with two hands yanked
brush rollers from your hair.

I can' t let anyone see me like this,

you said. I said no one would care.
You kept tugging – begged me for a
comb. There were rollers rolling around
the dashboard, falling to the floor,
when I screeched onto Hospital Road.
They punctured your chest,
inserted a tube,
inflated your lung,
while I watched and worried, hoping
they wouldn't make a mess
of your perfect curls.

Squamscott

Dave Kellam
Exeter, NH

The River breathes.
Slow draws swell the channels,
And embrace rock, bouy and boat.
Under an ancient contract it sucks life upstream,
Resuscitating the shallows, nourishing the shores.

The inhalation brings herring, a siege of lithe marathoners,
Trading safety for the chance to shutter and be spent.
Great blues and haggard men stalk the dizzy ones,
Ending a phenomenal four year winning streak.

When the River relaxes and the gray bottom appears,
Briny things stick between dark, stony teeth.
Gulls pick and pick and pick,
Laughing manically at their good fortune.

Glaciers retreated and gave birth to the River.
It rhythmically persists,
Slowly earning the trust of fish and fowl,
Barely noticing angler, miller, student or tourist.
It lulls the town and provides a mooring,
For a community to grow.

Old Road

Virginia Holder
Danville, NH

A century ago
Old road led the way
For carriage or sleigh,
A rider or runner by night or day
To homestead rustic,
Where generations lived and died;
Wilderness embraced
In natural beauty:
Cattle grazing on the hill
A farmer plowing – planting,
His fertile land to till.
Trees to tap for maple sap
Water buckets to be filled
Nourishment found in a milkweed pod
As farmer rests from turning sod.

Country kitchen the gathering room,
Venison stew in black iron pot
Fabric woven on grandma's loom
Homemade toys – no plaza to shop,
Babies born in borning-room
Infant's cradle to quietly rock.
No nursing home for the aged.

Homestead – stalwart midst pasture and field
Where all family needs are met,
For young and old,
Here conceived – Here
Finally laid to rest.

Old Road leads the way – today
Passing abandoned fields
Through wooded trails
Great pines and birches
Reaching for the sun.
Berries in season
Sturdy roots surviving,
A road pressed by hooves, wheels
And ancient runners;
Paved by travelers
Heavy hearted – or gay,
History inscribed – never to be read
As modern man retracts –
Noting clues along the way –
pondering his folk of yesterday.

Riverine Music
Nancy Hubbe
Durham, NH

The rhythm of the tides pervades the town,
Affording Exeter a longer view
Than its own history or schools' renown
Or ancient sites or artifacts can do.

Above the tides, the rapids' descant sings,
Bubbling past joys and troubles of our time,
Eloquent with wordless murmurings,
Joining the tides to mirror the sublime.

"Riverine Music, Bird's Eye View" by Nancy Hubbe

Snow in the Forecast

Gordon W. Johnson
Exeter, NH

Oh what a terrible morning!
There's white everywhere at dawning.
The snow is as high as a giraffe's brown eye,
And it's stretching right up to touch the sky!

It looks so pretty when it's coming down,
But we've got trouble when it hits the ground!
It's so hard to walk, it's even harder to see.
The landscape so white, you squint & say, "Gee!"

You listen to the forecast & hear the warning,
"Six inches more by tomorrow morning!"
On go the mittens, boots and warm hat,
On top of the snow suit, got it down pat!

Then it's shovel a path & clean off the car.
Can Spring be two months away? Really that far?
Grin and bear it, what else can we do?
Farmer's Almanac told us: **THEY KNEW!!**

"Haunted Wood" by Kitty Clark

Wentworth Hall........1957
Kate Leigh
Rye, NH

The family lands at my grandparents' for Christmas.
Moving back north from a year in Sarasota, Florida.
Nana and Grandad in Wentworth Hall; he, a dorm father.
We four children fly like banshees through hallowed halls.
Eternally long, rows of closed doors on either side.
We count and hide, duck into forbidden rooms
Studded with velvet armchairs, full bookshelves.
Smells of must and tweed. Solitary, silence,
Surrounded by tombs of learning, suffocated
By education, the absence of students.

Christmas break. Reality suspended. No
Crowds of boys in blazers. We read
Classics, fingertips on dust jackets,
Absorb Beethoven symphonies
Through our pores. We play cards
On Oriental-carpeted floors,
Sleep in high metal beds, with starched
Pillowcases and counterpane spreads.
Scent of lavender and soap boxes, jumbled
In a wooden-doored hallway closet.

Outside, great wingwide vistas of brick
Buildings, grass lawn, green expanses yawn.
We race and run each other down,
Then pound to get in as chill snow fell.
Warm indoors, my Nana's mantle
Holds ceramic Mrs. Tiggywinkle with her iron.
Above my head, treasures perch on a shelf
Over licking flames, promises of presents,
Stories of a giant's favorite cheese, and
Granny Glitten's candy mittens.

Now brush our teeth against sugarplums
And straightaway to bed.
The glass transom above each door
Leans open to pass the heat.
As eyes close, we ponder Santa
In the pulse of echoed space.

Front Street View

Sandra Tobin Mahoney
Portsmouth, NH

Just this side
of the Other side
of the tracks

His parents had been setting
him in the second story window
for weeks now, for show.
He waved at friends.

> *It's not by business…*
> *perhaps tomorrow*
> *I might call*

Then, late mourning in early autumn
I saw the toddler fly…
   Slowly…..
            Slowly……
                      Slowly
to the pavement.

Gameday

Gary Mann
Norridgewock, ME

Jammed thumbs, sprained ankles wrapped with that great white tape
Pre-game warmup, sharp and focused. Toss the coin and shake.
The Anthem sung. A kick-off run. Wound up, the huddle breaks.
> One knuckle on that soft game grass
> In that old familiar stance.
> Each play, teammates giving a hundred percent
> Remembering always our opponent's intent
> It'll sting through the pads, sometimes, just a bit,
> Hurts the other, too—and so we don't quit.

I never could hear the sounds of the band once on the field and playing.
So much to attend to,
There's whistles and what the referees and players are saying.
On cue I sail like a diesel down rails; nothing less is what is expected.
Sunshine or rain, each player moving the train;
Persistence makes us respected.
We learn to read the other team; sense what they're about to do.
Some telling by where they look, lean, or stand.
Conversely, too, we must hide our hand.
Our coaches strategize, call plays that fool.
Our "Do or Die" mettle's not our only fame.
We wipe out the toughest teams, all just the same.
> One last memory as I'm bending your ear:
> We earned our jackets as a result of this day.
> Jackets given by Exeter friends, by the way,
> Not passed to the team in the State's common way.
> I allude to this for one simple reason
> On our jackets, our patch read, "Undefeated Division III."
> Yes, we decisively, definitely beat Bishop G.,
> The team crowned "State Champs" that particular year
> In the very last game of the season.

On the Removal of
The Diseased Elm from the Exeter Playing Fields

Rex McGuinn
Exeter, NH

The high grand Elm realized
the promise of its seed on the green field
with its pitcher's mounds and soccer goals.

It had once been the focus of a lesson
on Aristotle, where under its limbs
the instructor explained entelechy.
More often it was the tree itself
under which faculty exercised their rescued greyhounds.

Now against a sky made in the Age of Leád
trucks surrounded its trunk.
Only a few come to share the skeletal shame
of two last limbs reaching high,
all else cut away,
the death of chaotic symmetry.

Now words must fill the absence
of the great tree. They do the job best
in a world of absence. The word "tree"
is not a tree. The word Elm
cuts away grand limbs
in ramifications of each private memory.
So alumni imagine love and grief
when they hear the word, the spoken Elm,
the tree itself absent in March wind
blowing new white snow over dirty banks
of ice lingering while games go on indoors.

Rex McGuinn (1951-2002) was born in Hendersonville, North Carolina. He died suddenly from a heart attack on a beautiful Saturday afternoon while out on a training run for a marathon. Rex was a beloved, award-winning teacher of English at Phillips Exeter Academy from 1987 until his death. Among his many passions were Shakespeare, basketball and other sports, Habitat for Humanity, the theater, and poetry. He was devoted to his wife Margaret, with whom he loved to travel, birdwatch, and entertain at home. His warmth, intelligence, and infectious humor are remembered by all who knew him.

Saltpetre and Robert Frost
Jack McCarthy
Arlington, WA

At the boys' school I attended
we all believed the legend
of saltpetre in the mashed potatoes.
The salt was said—as when grease fires
flare in kitchens—to deaden the unruly
flames of forbidden sexuality.
But if saltpetre was there truly,
it was notable for ineffectuality.

This was the same school where
they brought in some big names-
Oppenheimer, Robert Frost,
legends in their own lifetime—
to spend a week on campus in
the "Visiting Fireman" program.
They'd sit with us in class
and meet with small groups

of hand-picked students—
myself included—who,
with all roads open, asked
only the most general questions,
the vaguest of directions.
Frost was old, gentle,
white-haired, ever respectful
of us, but had an air as though

always holding back a laugh
at some constant running joke
as if his intercourse with us
was just a playful fragment
of an ongoing dialogue
between two lovers, the way
you'd sit a three-year-old
on your knee and tell her

in her mother's hearing she
would be even more beautiful
than her mother, if only such
perfection were possible, and the words
are heartfelt appreciation,
the hyperbole is slight;
the lovers' joke is in
the indirection.

Some people ask me today,
"Why do you write poetry?"
Sometimes I say to them
that it's my Irish blood;
other times I tell them how I shook
the feathery, parchment hand of
Robert Frost when I was seventeen,
maybe something took.

But if I say that, they ask
why I lost so many years
before I started writing.
Sometimes I answer that I counted cost;
other times I tell the legend
of saltpetre past, highlighting
the fact that it and Frost
kicked in at last

about the same time.

Shade on the Ice of the Exeter River
Rex McGuinn
Exeter, NH

Loquacious river in black ice
    of subterranean afternoon
like undulating smoke that speaks
    from a steamy winter fire,
sinuous through dark forests of
    December, cedar shade etched out
by paths white with freezing rain
    tapping while the river booms
in the sun-dying day—

a spirit, they say, wanders
    in the silence of limbs
and whispers in the tapping
    of falling ice,
whispers of a bend where
    cedars break and the
river has no bed, bottomless
    as the sky is deep into
wrinkled wrists of cloud.

Ask the ice-men in their shacks
    of a bend a mile beyond
the town, if they have heard
    the spirit whisper of the years,
the pickerel years, the age of jays,
    the dynasty of hares with
hieroglyphs across the snow—

there are those who have
    read the hieroglyphs of
hare feet, those who know this ghost
    in green branches after solstice
laced with delicate cotton sleeves.

Water Street Bookstore
Barbara Tuxbury McNeill
Exeter, NH

I will read and read and read what's written
In all places, bookmark will leave this page
With good imprint, writers live here-near
Nash, Frost, Millay, Whittier are close by, hear
Local American writers whittling their craft

Deboning inadequacies silently, absorbing
A best seller or something from any shelf
The fast and furious stroking inkwell quill,
The slowly methodical pendulum will,
Strike someone regardless of age –
Inspire ideas – audacity pricking fingers

The intensity of emotions running high
Here we go merry go round Main Street
Family town, U.S.A. writers will meet
The urge can't be helped-must write
Fulfilling need doesn't end one plight

Plot needs another circumstancial chance
Hanging wallpaper just so so plumb
From below looking up this business
Sign, signing seacoast authors greatness
Publishing quality, Water Street Bookstore…

A Sudden Gathering
Bob Moore
East Kingston, NH

As strange as she appeared
Without disguise or warning,
A visitor was spotted
in town the other morning.

More lifelike than a story
Or a camera could describe,
She rambled through the streets
And felt a growing vibe.

While others gathered 'round
Gazing in suspense,
She galloped down the sidewalk
In her own defense.

She slipped into the river
Like a submarine,
And pretty soon her furry head
Was all that could be seen.

The news traveled quickly
As it always does,
And other figures came
To check out where she was.

Local town observers
Called the local news,
And local town policemen
Call in morning crews.

She left the town compelled
To guess from where she came.
Was she from the northland?
Had she lost her way?

Or was she just returning
To an old ancestral home,
Before these streets were built
When moose were free to roam?

But visits as they come
Like a passing song
Leave a town to realize
What she knew all along.

A river is a haven.
A river can be crossed.
A river is the best course
To follow when you're lost.

The dew and you

Evan Mousseau
Exeter Student

As I walked on one spring morn,
My eyes fell upon the scenery
The beads of dew which magnify
The brightness of the greenery.
And as those drops fell to the ground
They formed a common bond
With others all around them
Upon pavement and on lawn.
Slowly did these droplets grow
Into a tiny trickle
That flowed in all directions,
Since not a drop was fickle.
And soon these water snakes grew too
Until they formed a stream
Which caught the morning sunlight with
A glimmer and a gleam.
I followed stream into a wood
Where it became a river
And wondering where it would go next
I followed every quiver
Of the wet road
That led me to
A pond with waters
Simmering blue.
'Twas such a sight of elegance
That nature lay at hand
And what a way to teach the world
The lesson oh so grand:
Each person makes a difference
Even if it's just a drop
For in the end your efforts
Will carry you to the top.

Resting On The Academy Library Lawn

Karen Nelson
Newton, NH

A place to be, to hear,
to weave the mind's reed baskets,
fill them with Bach's flute sonatas
wafting from the library windows
above.

Yeats heard these sounds
"in the deep heart's core." How deep,
how far in to find the loss, which one,
which glass bowl does rainwater fill
to the brim? We dance to escape from,
to loosen our heart strings,
or apron strings.

Rest now, lie down, look up,
see sky filter something you can't
calculate. How many leaves make
an umbrella to shelter you and him?

Adolescents perfume their mating dance,
butterflies do it in mid-air,
we dance the mating dance of the eyes,
a finely tuned balance.
Tree limbs sway above our heads
where we walk soundless,
feeling arced wood beneath
our bare feet as we spin out
into color, the shape of canopy,
green, linden blue, yellow, trees.

Green light spills over
into summer's shadow.
How many linden trees will it take
to fill your life's container
to the lip with leaves?

Boards and Blades

An Ode the 603 Skate Club and Ethan

Karen Noonan
Exeter, NH

Boards and blades
We want our way.
It's freedom that we seek.

Cement and steel
Roads and rails
That's where we reach our peak.

    But society says
    Grunge no more!
    They see us as rebels
    But against what?

    Our pants down to here
    Our caps upon our heads
    Button downs we aren't
    But we're your kids!

    We're loyal to friends
    Our family we love
    Just let us skate
    It makes us feel so great!

Boards and blades
We want our way.
It's freedom that we seek.

Cement and steel
Roads and rails
That's where we reach our peak.

"603 Skate Club" by Nick Veinot

The Ioka Theatre

Debra Nowak
Stratham, NH

Owner Jimmy Blanco courts no fools and you better respect that.
No lanky legs swing over his red velvet ropes, no disorderly
conduct in line at the old soda fountain's concession stand.

Sorrow of old buttered kernels and years of sweat are soaked
into the red vinyl seats. Between popcorn and Milk Duds
screen lovers fall back into each other's arms, bombs explode over

strafed villages, and poor Bonnie Blue lies dead in Rhett Butler's
cradling arms. Sergeant Elias gets up again and again, his arms flung
out at his side like some crazy Christ on the cross as the chopper lifts

higher and higher. The projection room's hot, noisy as hell
and two months ago some poor kid's finger was torn right off
in a 35mm's gyros. This is where Frankie first French-kissed

Annette up in the musty balcony. Where Johnny gathered courage
to place a sweaty palm around Katie's bare shoulder. Where so much
sadness unfolds as Virginia Woolf fills her pockets with stones,

walks into eternity's unforgiving sea, sinks into a silvery sheen
of speechless water that swallows a woman whole. The audience always
claps at the end. House lights come up, credits roll by, Adam and

Rachel still hold hands. Everyone's startled by the lobby's bright light.
Shoulders hunch against the cold. Rain falls as if heaven's unstoppered
its counterfeit joy. Pelts us as we dash headlong to the cold car.

The Klan in Exeter
Halloween, 1989
Pat Parnell
Stratham, NH

When the kids came to his house

for Trick or Treat,

he wore his white sheet

and pointed hood,

black eyeholes gaping,

to give them candy.

My Son Adam
Debra Nowak
Stratham, NH

Takes the Amtrak train from Exeter, 3 times a week to school, even though
he hears his name spoken when no one's there,
overhears the railway agents call him asshole.

And one sunny Friday he was certain the world was going
to be taken over by aliens, huge insects,
and somehow he was supposed to save us.

His hands shake from all his medicine. He ambles onto the subway,
like a big bear. Headphones smashed to his ears to drown out the voices.

The subway grinds to a halt. The conductor hollers "Brookline"
and he hurries off.

He is the bravest person I know.

He says, "I'm a beginner at everything."

I am frustrated by his slowness, by how he gobbles his food, how weekly
he quits cigarettes, how he's been doled out so much trouble.

He's mental health's displaced refugee, garrisoned in a long indifferent line.
His mind's a war-torn territory. Israel and Palestine's unforgiving
blood-bathed hands.

He often thanks me for small favors; Newport cigarettes, his favorite
dinner of medium-rare steak and potatoes,
a quick trip to the constant nearby ocean.

It's hard being such an impatient jerk with him.
Every day I pray for more patience, to speak only kind words,
to leave my sarcasm back inside my big mouth where it belongs.

He imagines he hears me call him bad names. Stupid. Jerk-off.
Hears me tell him he's going straight to hell on the fast train.

I pray that he won't be so afraid, that he'll get better.
I pray for guidance to signal the path he is to follow.

He dreams of being on the cover of Rolling Stone,
that soon he'll find a girlfriend, that his symptoms will go away.

I pray for miracles I no longer believe in.

He drags on cigarettes, as though he's inhaling all the poison
of the goddamn world. Ready to do battle with whatever is evil
and waits for him, waits for us all.

Cycling 101
On the Widening of Route 101, Exeter Segment
Pat Parnell
Stratham, NH

The glacier brought these boulders,
left them piled in billows of hills.
It scooped out the valleys, muddied the wetlands,
and went away.

Now another force breaks up the boulders,
levels the little hills, fills the valleys,
drains the wetlands.

> *Every valley shall be exalted*
> *and the mountains and hills made low*
> *the crooked straight*
> *and the rough places smooth*

Biblical injunction for highway improvement,
but no Messiah is coming.
Only tour busses, SUVs, pickup trucks, motorcycles,
and wide-load halves of houses, hauled
for instant homes.

One day the glacier will return,
break up the asphalt and pile it into hillocks,
scoop out new valleys.

And a scrim of soil settle here
and white pine and maple slide their roots
deep among the new boulders

a kingfisher catch tadpoles
in a new little pool.

Here

Jean Pedrick
Brentwood, NH

Here, he must have said,
having climbed the hill from the east,
the slope so gradual he'd not have known
he climbed until it opened to the western slope.

Here I will raise my house, he said,
and to the south my barn, and there
to the east and south clear pasturage,
and here will go apple orchard, here the ample
garden, and here by her window (when I find her)
golden honeysuckle and the damask rose.

And here black velvet berries, and here
(where they are) blue grapes, and all will stand
three hundred years or more, and I will call it
Gordon Hill, for myself, I, Alexander Gordon
thrall of fortune, alive, free, safe–
albeit hurtled far from England by O. Cromwell
to this 'pleasant seat'.

The Legacy Behind the Man
Marsha Pelletier
June 2003
Dover, NH

Strangely familiar the house on Epping Road I pass,
With little more than a backward glance at shutter P's
Hung neatly plumb outside the window glass I see.
Rich the green earth gives birth to Concord grapes,
Blueberry buckles, and fresh sun-buttered corn.
Rarer still, Baldwin apples fill trees that lean
Awaiting their time beyond worth cut clean.
Yet, Joe's shadow still sits near a roadside stand
Long past food free for the taking, the artisan,
Just so, the heart of a generous man.
So when the tidal water runs to park shore
The rowing crew pulls currents more
Of his life passing in a single wet dipped wooden oar.
Round the bandstand cycled music overflows
Live for the living memory listening,
That the crowd would wave back knowing
This was their beloved Exeter in tribute bestowing.
Among them a stranger still welcome in these parts
To their annual ritual speeches drifting
As Old Home Week cannons fires once more
To some distant train that signals passing.
Who would ever think, the same train
Would carry your grandson to this place
Where your gentle spirit lived and hammered.
You would have been proud had you known the path he took.
Perceptively smiling, Joe silently turns a comfortable stroll
Uphill to the Academy where all familiar souls go
To the sound and smell of freshly cut wood
Forming bookshelves, whose contents behold greatness.
Books to be respected, touched, and held
As your grandson opens new worlds in yours,
All the while knowing, true greatness comes in building
The cut of the wood, and the cut of the man.

Grapevine
Charles Pratt
Brentwood, NH

Last spring when he came to tell me he was dying,
He brought in a small green tub a grapevine dug
From the trellis behind his barn. "I thought you might like this,"
He apologized. "But it's puny. It may not survive."

It was already dead when I took him the photo to show
How I'd planted it down by the vine whose grapes Robert Frost
Is said to have favored. Withering on his sofa,
He smiled through his stubble and gave me a poem to read him.

I'd done what I could for my friend. It was for me
That this spring I took a cutting from his vine
Three buds long, and buried it two buds deep.
And now the top bud is bulging, preparing to burst,

While underground, I imagine, roots extend
A tenuous research into loam and clay.

Tracks

Charles Pratt
Brentwood, NH

Trailing an earlier skier through the pines,
I stop where he stopped, at a sudden stone:

SUSANNAH HOLMAN
wife of
JOSEPH BROWN
1785-1812

(Joseph Brown is carved as square and deep,
As if to say he has to bear more weight
Of years, pain, guilt to judgment); and then a footnote,
So low he's scraped the snow away to read

also an infant daughter

in italics, nameless.
We pause together, leaning on our poles.
Rest, Susannah Holman, from your hard delivery.
Rest, infant daughter. And wherever your grave may be,
Rest, Joseph Brown. The tracks lead smoothly on.

Raining

Ashley Rhodes
Exeter Student

The rain has begun to fall
and I am without an umbrella
It doesn't matter anymore
I was already drenched
before it had started to storm

The lightning will strike
I am left standing alone
I will be struck down
It is inevitable
I watch it all flash before my eyes

The winds change so quickly
One could get left behind
within the angered winds
and the melancholy tears
It all starts with one dark cloud

It teases the innocent hearts
that only hope for clear days ahead
I remain in the warm moments
and now I have been left behind
The rain always comes at the most inconvenient of
Times

I see it everywhere
Everything is drowning
It's drip, drip, dripping on my patience
I've seen the forecast for tomorrow
The worst has yet to come.

Making Marks
Elizabeth Reiter
Exeter, NH

Drew pictures of themselves as their mark.
Came river instead of forest: the Lamprey, Great Bay,
Squamscott and Piscataqua.
Much easier by far.
Two bridges, String Bridge, set logs or stringers across.
Great Bridge-*great* by comparison.

Only 6000 people! Why? Because Exeter manufacturers
And the Academy *Kept. Them. Out.*
Not long ago, nothing but a shoe shop, two shoe shops and a mill.
A shoe shop, two shoe
shops, and a mill. Sent fabric to Asia and Egypt…

The river has alewifes-Bait for big fish.
Just round the corner is where the rivers meet.

We're losing New England. Construction and stores.
We're losing New England. Deer and more deer.
I am not sure there are other animals,
Nocturnal animals…I am not sure.

Higgins Ice Cream Parlor…that was the big highlight.
The rest was woodlands and dairy farms.
Woodlands and dairy farms. You missed the Higgins generation.

After picking strawberries, I would run to Jenny Diner's.
I was her official candy taster.
She was wonderful, she was wonderful.
I can still taste it…nothing like homemade stuff
with a lot of TLC.

A lot of soul is dying here.
I used to know a lot of people you could talk to,
But a lot have passed away.
Those who are left are suspicious—

Do you know the Gilman House?
My buddy, Buddy Chase lived there.

Daniel Webster roomed there. There was a tunnel.
"Who dug it?" I asked.

Writing on the windowpanes, jump in the tunnel, run from attack.
And they called, "You can't go Joe—you can't go Joe.
The timbers are rotting out,
Timbers are rotting out."

Mr. Chase, he had an attic chocked full of arrowheads.
He'd remove the stones and they'd keep pushing up.

There was a little wooden hut with a little burning wood stove.
Mr. Damsel worked there for 70 years, and I'm not exaggerating.
He would take a hose with water and sprinkle it on the ice.
Made sure it was smooth. Smooooth ice.

I said, "Let's go back to 5th grade when we had 75 boys;
Course lots of them had to work.
We invite all of them and their wives to the reunion.

25 cents to skate for 2 hours. Then they got lights,
Lights for night skating.
We thought that was **big** technology. Lights for night skating—

We want to maximize everything. We all meet at 12 o'clock,
In autumn, at Yokens for
lobster.

The leaves are just right. The leaves are just right.

We do a lot of reminiscing. Reminiscing is a wonderful thing.
Nobody gets hurt.
Get everybody in the act. Have a lot of fun.

River Tide

Ron Roberts
Stratham, NH

MORNING HAZE FILTERS TO SOFTEN AND EDGES THE ORANGE GLOW
WAVES OF GREEN MARSH GRASS STANDS CALM AND STILL
THE HEAT DRAWN BREEZES WILL SOON BRING ABOUT SWAY TO FRO
ECHOES THE WINTER WREN AS HE FIFES HIS WARBLING TRILL
AN INSTANT IS SLACK THE WATER BEFORE THE EBB FOR IT'S REACHED ITS FLOW

BOUND AND HARNESSED THE RIVER'S BANKS ARE ITS THILL
FOR EACH SLIGHT RIPPLE THERE REFLECTS A SPARKLE
IF STILL IN TIME WE WILL CREATE NO WAKE
A DISTANT CROW'S ENDLESS PRATTLE
HERE TO BE MOVED BY THE MOTIONLESSNESS IF WE LET IT TAKE
FOR ITS WORKING WATERWAYS LONG SINCE TRAVERSED WITH PADDLE

WHERE RIVERS CONVENE BAYS TO OCEANS THEY MAKE
THE WHISPERING SILENCE OF CALM WE LONG TO FILL OUR MIND
BUT ONLY IF WE STAND WITNESS TO THE EBB OF A MOON TIDE
AND GRASP THE LOOSE END AS TIME WILL UNWIND
AS LIFE WITH ALL FROM NARROW TO WIDE
WE RUSH TO GATHER AND DEPOSIT THE DELTA OF MANKIND
IF ONLY ONCE JUST WITNESS THE TIDE

The Traces of History
Harvey Shepard
Exeter, NH

Has the past and its imprint vanished?

In the mirror I see my father's face,
the curve of his nose, full head of graying hair,
mother's taut neck muscles and watchful look.
What is more present and persistent
lies beneath, unseen.

In this prosperous town, antique cars are Sunday fun –
horses wait in stables and unplowed fields,
not in the streets; soldiers in Revolutionary dress
battle only at Independence Museum celebrations.

Perhaps it's on Water Street –
the 1770 Kimball Building or 1860 Janvrin's Block –
the bandstand and churches, Phillips Exeter Academy,
the big-screen Ioka's 1915 Mayer Building,
or in the shoe and woolen mills
converted to stores and condominiums.

But is there more – does the past
matter now to how we live
in old Revolutionary Exeter?

There are mornings I wake – and for a moment
could be any age, with no history,
no links to the past. But soon
the groove of thoughts, my body's reality
and whole lifestory reassert themselves
in consciousness – and in what I carry
but do not know.

Exeter

Gloria Dibble Pond
Woodbury, CT

Empearling with memory's nacre
Ecstasies, quarrels, loneliness, loves,
Inside Langdon Hall seasoned citizens
See through their glasses darkly
A slender Great Blue Heron
Stalking fish, stabbing neighbors,
Twisting, easing, crookedly swallowing,
Then standing still, tall, waiting.

Handkerchief Factory

Charlene Mary-Cath Smith
Manchester, NH

the beginning

When kleenix
Suggested
'Don't put a cold
   in your pocket'

of

the end

"Autumn Colors" by Annick Bouvron-Gromek

Boathouse

Norma Segal
Durham, NH

Painted lady
in an old town
tarted up
defies leaden skies
windows arched
disdainful eyebrows
she speaks of summer,
shouting boys,
rattling sculls
rowing the Swampscott
where Yankees kept their powder dry.

"Across the River" by Helen Hazen

Walking the Exeter Woods in Late Fall

Harvey Shepard
Exeter, NH

Ah – no bugs!
Gone, like false ambition
that aims to please, impress.
The frantic activity of summer
past – now a stillness, quiet
enough to hear the underlife.

Squirrels and chipmunks gather
their winter store. Bluejays,
woodpeckers still at work
among abandoned nests.
The ground a carpet of oak leaves
decorated with dry branches.

I look from the sunny path
into dark wood shade,
envious of the tall pine growth
serene in eternal greenness.
Red berries of the mountain ash
seem too new and bright for this season.

The beauty of many shapes is revealed,
hidden forms, twistings of a long growth.
Ahead, a black dog with no master
turns me to a route along the river.
A drowsy bee, even the echo of gunshots
can't break my mood: for now, this day,
this path is enough.

on the Road from Manchester
Charlene Mary-Cath Smith
Manchester, NH

   in this 21st century
   as I ride through Exeter
Rich with bricks that whisper charm
Bricks that salute history
Forty plus years later
It's the fondness of brownies I recall
Not the Amoskeag daredevils
Who dive and swim on creaky film
   in January's freezy degrees
   but those
One gobbles in junk food ecstasy

 …Viewing the Raymond village sign
Our anticipation rose, the glorious
Chewy-nut feed just a morsel away
They stood beckoning in the showcase
Purest ingredients, these ample fudgy
Squares became a major contribution
   to our glad day
   at Hampton, its gleeful playground

…Today the town's purity lingers
No water diluting process
I carry armloads of 100% cotton
Skirts   blouses   what-have-you
Recycling the memories of a bygone era
Two Flights Down accompanied by
   the ghost
   of a Pleasant Street bakery
Red brick curvature evident, its smiley
Lip hung with chocolate crumbs
Wafting/weaving a childhood sweetness
Through Exeter's winding streets.

Moe

Colin Supple
West Yarmouth, MA

For a fearsome friend
the jail cries out its lonely ache,
a hospital hostaged to death;
a bleak blight of days…

Our father who art in Exeter
now the presence of absence,
a serious silence
surrounds…

His therapy of love's little things,
always allowed anything good;
courage crouches in the shadows
waiting to be called in…

A community of compassion
at core, hear-less and head-less;
but our face of faith rises afresh,
with him…

Trolling for Ideas
Olive Tardiff
Exeter, NH

Writers and fisherfolk are much the same;

We cast our lines abroad with careful aim.

Indeed our fondest aspirations match;

We're hoping for a nibble, or better yet a catch.

Whatever course our earnest offering traces,

We pray our lines will fall in profitable places.

Daydreaming at the Beach

Kelsey Tierney
Exeter Student

I walk along the shore, there's a gentle breeze
It follows me and cools my hot face and neck
The sky is calming blue with scattered wispy clouds
My feet carry me on, and my mind is at ease.

My toes squish into the grainy sand
Salt spray comes up and spits in my face
I see an old and forgotten boat a little ways up ahead
It seems to be sagging with neglect on the land

The tide comes in chasing my bare feet
The sun is now sinking below the horizon
Seagulls soar and dive looking for food
I see my sister in the distance, she I came to meet.

Then the both of us walk the beach
My arm linked with hers
I look up at the sky and think
The ocean shows you many things, but it can also teach.

Layers of Magic

Kelsey Tierney
Exeter Student

The sun dances across my face
The wind teases my hair
The waves crash against the rocks
Without a single thought or care

The moon glimmers through the trees
An owl hoot I hear
A coverlet of leaves way up above
Swaying silently in the breeze

There are so many starts I see
But I cannot count them all
I never feel alone at night
They glow with such intensity

They shine, glimmer, and glow on me
They spread a layer of magic on me
The moon, and sun, and stars I see.

At the Paloma Unit
Langdon Place of Exeter

Maren C. Tirabassi
Portsmouth, NH

A humming bird hovers at the azaleas
outside his window.
Macula gone, his head swings
like fly-fretted livestock
to catch its sweet comma
in peripheral vision.

He does not remember who we are,

but rapid wings and pink flowers
go deep to stir
Tennessee honeysuckle
reminiscences,

though any recollection now
sucks out the fearful times…
a lynching he saw as a boy,
mountain feuds,
the Bulge, Dachau.

We sign ourselves out
at the ledger on the nurses' station,

(they call it elopement when folk wander off)

and walk to the pond outside the fence
stocked with the painted sun
of goldfish.
Gingerly, with cane and arm,
we circumnavigate.

There are other fathers and daughters,
mothers and sons on benches.

A blue heron stands—
rich as Midas.
It, too, is beautiful, merciless.

Here and There: "Old Home Day,"
Exeter, New Hampshire, June 26, 1982

David Weber
Exeter, NH

This old Yankee town sets its own dates,
but from year to year I forget them.
So when the first charge of powder burst
like a ship's shell in the darkening
sky behind our neighbor's house tonight,
I remembered the evening news,
the assault on Beirut, everyone
racing through crumbling streets, children
lying frightened in damaged hospitals.
My wife and child, knowing all along
that the Fourth comes early here, cheered
with excitement and trotted over to the park
by the river, where everyone
was watching the festive streaks and flashes
as they arced out over the familiar water,
lighting the local sky with sudden spangles
of gold, white, red, and filling the summer air
with the shouts of innocent bombs.

Market Day in Exeter

Margaret Reed Whitney
Nashua, NH

Drive East, and when you reach the place
where the river meets the sea
at Exeter,
on Thursdays in the summer,
you will come upon the town on Market Day.

All along the parkway
beside the estuary
bright umbrellas shade offerings of
tomatoes, apples, squash and flowers.
Jams and jellies glisten in jars of
captured summer sun,
alongside breads and cakes,
egg rolls, herbs and yarn,
and clever craftwork fashioned
in hours stolen from the fields.

Babies ride in royal splendor in their buggies.
Children dart among the browsers,
some tethered to their mothers' wrists.
Old folks tap their canes from booth to booth.
Women stroll in jeans or shorts or long, graceful skirts,
carrying baskets,
and here and there someone from a nearby office,
dressed for business,
adds a new dimension to the scene.

Everywhere the bountiful display,
the warmth of the sun,
the murmur of voices,
laughter,
the harsh cry of gulls,
and mingled aromas
create a feeling of content,
at the wealth of the harvest,
of plenty,
on Market Day in Exeter.

The Most Mispronounced Word In Exeter

Donald R. Young
Berwick, ME

Suppose you had to say,
"Evelyn Z-a-r-n-o-w-s-k-i", every day,
Or better yet, make the name,
"Benny Swiezynski" roll off your lips
In perfect harmony and cadence.
It wouldn't take you long to get it right,
And practice each component syllable
Into a recognizable name.

Those names were different from so many others,
But not so different that the Anglicized orthography
Prevented them from being pronounced correctly.
But the word that is most commonly mispronounced
Is a short, little word whose alphabet has left us,
And thus we say:
"Eye" "Ooh" "Kay" "Aah"

When in a time of greater elucidation
We would have been taught in Greek,
Long gone from required courses,
To utter with alliterative delight,
"Iota" "Sigma" "Kappa" "Alpha"

Which in its ancient splendor
Is a gift to us from Ptolemy
Whose voice and sound we should thus render:
The word is "Iska".
So frame it and let it fall
Full upon your ears
As it was meant to sound;

Nor try to parse this simple word
Into a simpler acronym
Which says, "I owe Kelly all".
Our debt is greater and to a nobler mind.

"String Bridge" by Bill Childs

Index to Titles and First Lines

A century ago, 50
A day in Exeter, 32
A humming bird hovers at the azaleas, 93
A place to be, to hear, 67
A Sudden Gathering, 64
After Thanksgiving, on High Street, 46
Ah – no bugs!, 87
Aloofes, 38
As I walked on one spring morn, 66
As strange as she appeared, 64
At MIT, they used an Oliver Smoot, 36
At the boys' school I attended, 60
At the Paloma Unit, 93

Before the Squamscott was the Squamscott, 38
Boards and blades, 68
Boathouse, 86
By the Squamscott in August, 44

Cycling 101, 74

Daydreaming at the Beach, 91
December Renaissance, 41
Down Near the Dock, 26
Drew pictures of themselves as their mark., 80
Drive East, and when you reach the place, 95

Empearling with memory's nacre, 84
Every village had its idiot. It wasn't, 15
Exeter, 16
Exeter, 84
Exeter Revisited, 20
Exeter's Night, 18

Ferdinand and Miranda in Exeter, 43
For a fearsome friend, 89
Front Street View, 57

Gameday, 58
Grapevine, 77

Handkerchief Factory, 85
Has the past and its imprint vanished?, 83
Here, 75
Here and There: "Old Home Day," Exeter…, 94

Here, he must have said, 75
Hoarfrost coats and cuffs, 29
How do I get there? Start at the Bandstand., 35
Huddled and walking fast, 42

I drive down the short, steep hill, 13
I leave the town landing, tired and discouraged., 27
I remember your eyes, full, 48
I took my class on a field trip, 30
I walk along the shore, there's a gentle breeze, 91
I will read and read and read what's written, 63
In Lieu Of Fathers, 22
in this 21st century, 88
In Thompson Gym, 28
In town, at the window—, 46

Jammed thumbs, sprained ankles wrapped..., 58
Just now, like a candle floating on a rippled pond, 21
Just this side, 57

King David of Exeter (fl. 1875-1885), 15

Last spring when he came to tell me he was dying, 77
Layers of Magic, 92
Listen, grizzled gray, sebum-flaked tom cat, 24
Loquacious river in black ice, 62

Machine Dreams, 19
Major Blake's Hotel, 31
Making Marks, 80
Market Day in Exeter, 95
Memorial Day in Exeter, 14
Memory Lane, 40
Moe, 89
Morning haze filters to soften..., 82
My Son Adam, 72

North of Boston, 29

Ode to the Lamprey, 34
Oh what a terrible morning!, 54
Old men in uniforms parade in Exeter, 14
Old Road, 50
On the Removal of the Diseased Elm from..., 59
On the Road from Manchester, 88
One day in July cool and warm, 23
Once you could take the trolley from my corner, 47
Our heroes were horses with names like, 22

Owner Jimmy Blanco courts no fools and..., 70

Painted Lady, 86
Peeps drilling on the flats, 44
Playing chess on the oil tablecloth at Sparky's, 20

Quaint little Exeter, my mother's hometown, 40

Raining, 79
Respect Starts with You, 24
Resting On The Academy Library Lawn, 67
Retired to their den, 43
River Tide, 82
Riverine Music, 52
RiverWoods' seasons, in haiku, 25
Rose Spring, 13

Saltpetre and Robert Frost, 60
Schooling, 30
Shade on the Ice of the Exeter River, 62
Snow in the Forecast, 54
Snow is Winter's gift., 25
Spring Prom, Exeter May 1947, 28
Squamscott, 49
Start at the Bandstand, 35
Strangely familiar the house..., 76
Summer Evening on the Squamscott, 27
Suppose you had to say, "Evelyn..., 96

Takes the Amtrak train from Exeter..., 72
Team Play in Autumn, 37
the beginning, 85
The Bridge at Exeter, 36
The dew and you, 66
The family lands at my grandparents'..., 56
The glacier brought these boulders, 74
The high grand Elm realized, 59
The Ioka Theatre, 70
The Klan in Exeter, 71
The Lamprey is a river, 34
The Legacy Behind the Man, 76
The Most Mispronounced Word In Exeter, 96
The Old Woman, 23
The rain has begun to fall, 79
The rhythm of the tides pervades the town, 52
The River breathes.,49
The sun dances across my face, 92
The Tavern by the River's Edge, 42

The time has come, 19
The Traces of History, 83
This old Yankee town sets its own dates, 94
This sun-locked, long wood dock, dotted..., 26
Three on an elevator, nose to nose, 31
Tracks, 78
Trailing an earlier skier through the pines, 78
Tribute to an Unknown Exeter Woman, 21
Trolling for Ideas, 90
Twelve below: sea smoke, 41
Twenty-minutes' tunneling through trees, 16

Used to be and Now, 47

Walking the Exeter Woods in Late Fall, 87
Water Street Bookstore, 63
Wentworth Hall……..1957, 56
What I wonder is: Were there some people, 32
When the kids came to his house, 71
While Our Lungs are Collapsing, 48
Wildly, the playful moon towers above me, 18
Wind shakes leaves loose to encounter the air, 37
Writers and fisherfolk are much the same, 90